SO THERE WE WERE... RIGHT IN THE THICK OF THE WOODS.

SO I TOOK IT UPON MYSELF TO ENSURE THEIR SAFETY.

A GROUP OF ASSHOLES DECIDED TO GO AFTER THE GIRLS...

SO, TO THAT END.

2

LONER LIFE IN ANOTHER WORLD

CONTENTS

Ch. 13	March of the Morons	001
Ch. 14	Encountering the Meatheads...	017
Ch. 15	I'm Gonna Crash! Gaaahhh!!!	029
Ch. 16	Old Farts Sighted! Let's Play It Safe!	041
Ch. 17	The Great Wolf Fiasco	055
Ch. 18	That's Me in the Corner, That's Me in the Spotlight	067
Ch. 19	Not Fair... Not Fair! These Other-Worlders Make No Damn Sense!	081
Ch. 20	Some Lonely Peace and Quiet	093
Ch. 21	Item Store? More Like "Major Bore"	105
Ch. 22	The Loner Life Was Easier in the Forest...	117
Ch. 23	It's Nerd Hunting Season	129
Ch. 24	Who, Me? I'm Just a Neet...	141
EXTRA BONUS STORY	The Tumultuous Tongue-Twisting Terror	157

THE NERDS HAD WARNED ME OF A CREATURE I'D YET TO ENCOUNTER.

Swish

AND THERE IT WAS...

Orc Lv 11

A WILD ORC.

DA-DUN

TOPPLE

Wow...

WH-WHAT?

WHAT KIND OF LEARNING EXPERIENCE WAS THAT! SUPPOSED TO BE?!

But how?

IT'S... DEAD?

BUT I THOUGHT IT HAD HIGH DEFENSE...

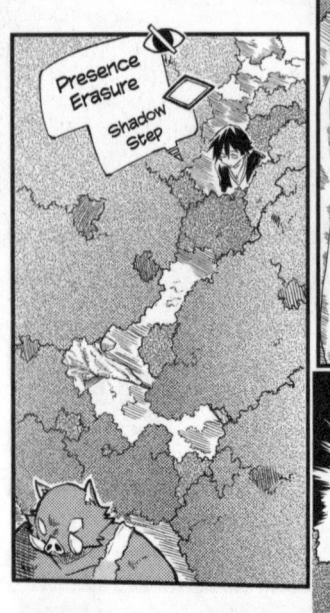

DAY 17

WAHOO!

Shing

ALL RIGHT!

WE'RE HEADING DEEPER INTO THE FOREST, SO PREPARE YOURSELVES!

I WANTED TO TELL YOU EARLIER, BUT I NEVER GOT THE CHANCE!

REGARDING MY SKILL...

HIJACK, RIGHT?

H-HUH?! HOW DID YOU KNOW?!

O-ODA AND THE OTHERS SAID THEY'D KEEP IT A SECRET...

THEY DIDN'T SAY ANYTHING. IT WAS PRETTY OBVIOUS.

Those boneheads didn't notice though.

W-WELL, IF YOU KNEW, WHY DID YOU COVER FOR ME? AREN'T YOU WORRIED?

SHOULD I BE? THE NERDS WEREN'T.

YET THE NERDS WEREN'T WORRIED KNOWING THAT, SO WHY SHOULD I BE?

UHM... WHAT DO YOU MEAN EXACTLY?

EXACTLY.

B-BUT...

IF I WANTED TO, I COULD STEAL ANYONE'S SKILLS.

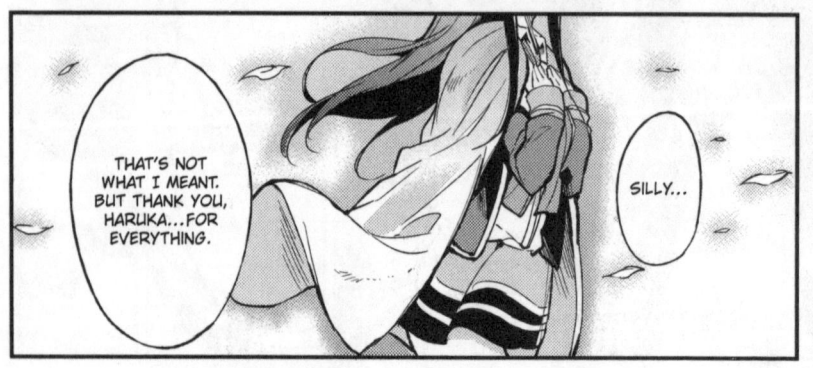

IT'S NOT MY FAULT! I DIDN'T DO ANYTHING!!!

WHOOSH!

THAT'S MOSTLY BECAUSE OF YOU, HARUKA.

THAT'S NOT WHAT I MEANT. BUT THANK YOU, HARUKA...FOR EVERYTHING.

SILLY...

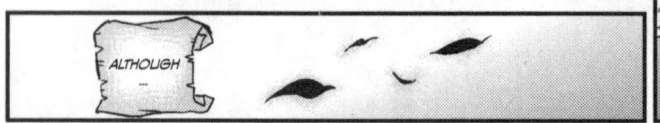

AND SOME BAD THINGS...

A LITTLE TOO MUCH HAPPENED.

WHY'D THEY HAVE TO STAMPEDE OVER ME LIKE THAT?!

S-Sorry...

...BUT IT ALL PAID OFF.

Chapter 17:
The Great Wolf Fiasco

H-HARUKA?! WHAT'S GOT YOU SO RILED UP?!

I JUST WOKE UP, IT'S TOO EARLY FOR THIS!

CITY OF OMUI

WOW, SO THIS IS OMUI!

IT SURE IS BUSTLING.

THE BUILDINGS ARE SOOO CUTE! THEY LOOK LIKE CUPCAKES!

I wonder if you can eat them...

Any tapioca pearls inside?

...I GUESS A STRICT DIET OF FISH AND MUSHROOMS BROKE THEM.

OH, C'MON, ANOTHER OLD MAN...?

CAN'T THE AUTHOR THROW A CUTE GIRL IN HERE SOMEWHERE?

GUILDMASTER

character

Fwiiish!

WHOA...

A-ALL RIGHT, THAT'S ENOUGH! COME BACK TOMORRAH!

DESPAIR

HUH? DO I NEED TO BRING IN MORE OR SOMETHING?

YEAH, LEMME JUST GET 'EM OUT FOR YOU...

WH-WHAT'S WITH ALL THESE? ARE YA JOKIN'?

WHAT?! YOU HAVE MORE?!

At least walk on your own...

HEY, HARU-KA!

THIS IS THE HOTEL THE GUILD SUGGESTED!

FINALLY MADE IT.

"I HONESTLY EXPECTED THIS TO LOOK MUCH TACKIER..."

"OH, HUH..."

"THEY WERE KINDA CRAPPY, SO I DOUBT I'LL GET MUCH... AH WELL, TIME TO NAP."

"WELP, NOW I JUST WAIT FOR THE MONEY TO ROLL IN FROM THE SPELLSTONE EXCHANGE."

"Where are you, Oda...?"

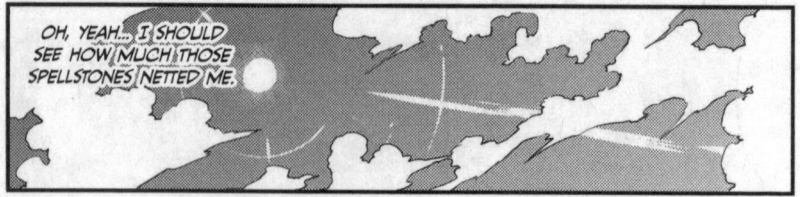

SO WE TOOK THE QUANTITY OF YER GOODS INTO ACCOUNT...

...AND TACKED ON THE REWARD FROM THE GREENWOLF QUEST!

THAT'S WHERE THE REAL MONEY CAME FROM!

LOOKS LIKE WE'LL BE ABLE TO LIVE THE GOOD LIFE FOR A WHILE, GIRLS.

GREAT! THEN LET'S GO BUY SOME SUPPLIES!

HURRAY!

Slacking off again! I'm sorry!!!

WELL, LATER!

'MEMBER...

I STILL OWE YA SOMETHIN' NICE, RIGHT?

YO, KID.

ARE YOU COMING WITH US?

HM, NOT SURE YET. I DON'T KNOW THE LAY OF THE TOWN.

OHOHO, HOW CAN I SAY NO TO A KATANA?!

Magically-enhanced Blade (FUNC REQ: LV 50)

MANA CUTTER

EVEN IF I CAN'T USE THE MAGIC PART YET, OWNING IT'S COOL ENOUGH...

CLATTER

H-HEY, KID... SHOPKEEP NEEDS TO CLOSE UP SOON...

AIN'T MUCH LIGHT LEFT...AND I'M PRETTY BORED...

...

CLATTER...

DAY 20

I'M BROKE...

BUT THERE'S SO MUCH I WANNA BUY...

Be frugal!

THE CLASS REP WON'T GIVE ME ANY POCKET CHANGE...

WE MANAGED TO SETTLE THE BILL AT 8 MIL...

BUT NOW I DON'T HAVE ANY CASH...

He's a bit... special.

PUSH

NO!

AND I CAN'T TAKE ON ANY QUESTS AT THE GUILD...

ODA?

WE'RE OFF!

DAY 21

WE'RE HEADED OUT ON OUR FIRST QUEST!

HEY, UH...

THE GIRLS ARE FULL-FLEDGED ADVENTURERS NOW, HUH... CAN'T SAY I'M NOT JEALOUS.

ABSO-LUTELY NOT!!!

At least, the bimbos did...!

I JUST THOUGHT I COULD HELP TRACK THEM DOWN.

I PROMISE I WON'T... YOU SPOTTED THE NERDS YESTER-DAY, RIGHT?

You made me really mad!

SCOWL SCOWL

SO YOU CAN TRY AND RUN AWAY FROM US LIKE YESTERDAY? NO WAY!

...CAN I COME WITH YOU?

PHOOEY...

I'M HOME FREE!!!

SWEET FREEDOM!!!

SNICKER

NOW I JUST RUN DOWN THESE ROADS...

DASH...

...AND CHASE DOWN ANY NERDS I SEE!

MAN, THAT WAS WAY EASIER WITHOUT THE GIRLS AROUND TO WORRY ABOUT...

...They really got in my way...

HM?

HMM?

CLANG
HEHEHEH...
TAKE THAT!

TYPICAL FANTASY WORLD FOR YA... Neat.

EVEN GOT BANDIT RAIDS GOING ON, HUH...

WE DON'T WANT NO WITNESS... THINK WE'LL LET YOUR FACE GET OFF SCOT-FREE?!

H-HUH...?

YOU DUMB-ASS JOCKS THINK YOU CAN BE WHITE KNIGHTS?

BACK OFF, BRO. YOU'LL GET TO THOSE GIRLS OVER OUR DEAD BODIES.

PFFT...

IF THAT'S HOW YA WANT IT!

To be continued...

The Tumultuous Tongue-Twisting Terror

  I didn't know what sparked this. Perhaps it was some sort of fanatical cult's influence. Maybe it was a stroke of mania... But the girls began speaking in a strange way all of a sudden.
  ""Peter Piper picked a peck of pickled peppers. A peck of pickled peppers Peter Piper picked. If Peter Piper picked a peck of pickled peppers? Where's the peck of pickled peppers Peter Piper picked? She sells sea shells by the seashore!""
  "What are you going on about, you pervs?! I'm gonna call the town guard or whoever else I need to report you to!
  ""...Why are you calling us pervs? We're just reciting tongue twisters to train our articulation and improve our lung capacity!""
  "I-I don't know, it just feels...dirty when you do it? Like it's wrong, somehow..."
  ""Well, we don't care! You try one!""
  "Uhh, okay... The city of Bangkok's full name is Krung Thep Mahanakhon Amon Rattanakosin Mahinthara Ayuthaya Mahadilok Phop Noppharat Ratchathani Burirom Udomratchaniwet Mahasathan Amon Piman Awatan Sathit Sakkathattiya Witsanukam Prasit. How's that?"
  ""You're talking way too fast! There's no way we can memorize that!""
  I had half a mind to believe they were cursing me, but I decided to trust in their claims that they were merely trying out some tongue-twisters.
  ""Don't hassle us anyway! We're practicing! The sixth sick

sheik's sixth sheep's sick! Round the rough and rugged rock the ragged rascal rudely ran! Nine nimble noblemen nibbling nuts!""

...No way, there's definitely something perverted about all this.

""Eve eating eagerly elegant Easter eggs! Ingenious iguanas improvising an intricate impromptu on impossibly impractical instruments!""

"Uhh… Picasso's full name is Pablo Diego José Francisco de Paula Juan Nepomuceno María de los Remedios Cipriano de la Santísima Trinidad Ruiz y Picasso! Something like that?"

""Wait, was it really?!""

"Hmm... That was more a fun fact than a tongue twister, huh."

Apparently, they were practicing tongue twisters because of their weapon skills. Doing this was some kind of unholy mixture of articulation, lung capacity training, and aerobic exercise.

"So you're practicing to better utilize your weapon skills?"

""Of course! Why else would we be doing this?!""

It seemed that, without proper training, fights were taxing both vocally and physically, and it only got worse as they trekked on. This one bandit apparently bit his tongue, rolled around, and became all pale and weird-looking due to cyanosis. It made me appreciate the art of shutting up and fighting.

"You always start with skill names first. You know what'll happen if you don't continue with lightning-fast articulation, don't you?"

""Yeah, we'll be forced to go on a diet instead!""

"Well, it's better than gorging yourselves and getting fa— No, nevermind, I didn't say anything! Oh yeah, I just remembered something that as thick with... GAAAHHH!!!"

"Watch whose legs you're, like, looking at when you say that!"

It was good of them to show enthusiasm about their potential weapon skills, but were aerobics the right way to get them?

That wouldn't suit their goal, would it?

"'These thousand tricky tongue twisters trip thrillingly off the tongue!'"

"Huh? You oka— Wait, no! That's it! I was watching 'cuz I was worried about the chubby chicks...all right?"

"'WHO'RE YOU CALLING CHUBBY?!'"

"Honestly, it takes more air just to talk to Haruka than it does to say these tongue twisters..."

"'If you notice this notice, you will notice that this notice is not worth noticing!!'"

"It's not my fault you girls ate so much... Er, nothing, I didn't say anything!!!"

Man, these bimbos can be really scary... Also, weren't inns in other worlds supposed to be the starting points for adventurers? Why were we getting endless tongue twisters instead?

"Hey, it's not like weapon skills are that difficult to say, right? I mean, the bandit was out of breath, but he didn't bite his tongue that much... Damn, you look really worn out!"

"'Nngh... You should've said that sooner!!!'"

I was pretty sure that weapon skills were mixed in with the attack themselves, and by activating them you turned your attacks into combat chants... The problem appeared to stem from the translations of this world's language getting all jumbled up.

"I remember when I was attacked by those bandits. They were yelling out their skill names, but I kept hearing stuff like 'Base,' 'Stratosphere,' and other nonsense like that. I wonder if our translation's on the fritz?"

At the very least, I definitely remembered them shouting something along those lines. This world sure has its share of mysteries!

"'Are you sure they were shouting skills in the first place?!'"

"Yeah, I think so! But this one guy yelled out '/ /' and 'www.' I was confused as hell! It's not like he was online, right?! So why'd he keep saying 'forward slash'?! Maybe he was just out of signal range."

""He'd have to be really far out!!!""

The mystery of the local language went deep, but the transferring of info it allowed was more or less perfect, save for a few confusing parts.

"I was thinking maybe the 'www' part meant 'World Wide Web,' but how would a bandit have knowledge of the internet to begin with?"

""I don't think that's what they were saying, Haruka!!!""

"Then what, were they members of a baseball club, and that was their code word for making a play or something?"

""I really don't think they wanted to play baseball either, Haruka!!!""

I might've found something out if I asked that nameless girl, but she came from a family who lived in a nameless area, so I had no way of finding her again! She talked about so much stuff that I'd basically forgotten it all already.

"Oh, I've got it! Maybe they were saying, 'Let's attack the first baseman and whack him out of the stratosphere! Whazam!'"

""What first baseman?! What are you even saying? And what's with the 'whazam' part?! You're being weird, Haruka!!! Anyway, back to the tongue twisters… Batter, runner, victor, clean sweep of the runners!!!""

"Aha! I've got it! They were planning a clean sweep of the first base!"

""That's definitely not the situation, Haruka! Uhm… Four fine fresh fish for you!!""

"Wait, four you say? Of course! The fourth out in baseball!

That means they were going to attack the first baseman and the ump!"

""What are you even saying?! And why are you so fixated on them attacking the first baseman?! Uhhm, let's try another… An arrow rarely reaches a ripping rope!!!""

"…Rope?"

""Y-Yes? What's wrong with that?!""

"No, nothing. Everyone has their own tastes and all that. You're perfectly free to be into rope and stuff… Just didn't expect you'd be the types to like being tied up."

""What are you talking about?! Why would we be tied up?!""

"Oh, so you'd rather tie me up?"

""NO!!!""

In the end, the language of this world was a funny thing. Sometimes I heard things that didn't quite feel right and had to piece together what was being said based on the context, though it all seemed like it didn't perfectly mesh into my native tongue like it should have.

""Who even started all this nonsense?!""

"Hm? Wasn't it the first baseman?"

""STOP TALKING NONSENSE, DAMN IT!!!

They had a good point though. I'd seen some raggedy old bandits, a middle-aged town guard, and quite a few other things in this world. But I hadn't seen a first baseman. Frankly, I hadn't even seen a baseball field!

Episode end.

Hey-ho! Bibi here! Thanks to all your support, I think my Manga Author skill definitely rose up to Level 2 this time around! Thanks everyone, you really helped me out! Now I just need to work on my Screentone and Line Drawing skills. We'll see if we can get me a nice level up by next time, guys! Maybe a cheat skill will finally show up and I'll really be able to let loose! It's more likely that I'll just rely on my assistants though. They're a pretty important part of all this! But I'm a loner... I don't think I can actually call them over, right? The Loner skill means you can't form a party, right?! Gaaah, Haruka sure is lucky. I wish I had some company right about now. Anyway, I might be an artist living my loner life in this world, but I promise to keep on drawing my best! Thanks for all your support so far, and see you next time!

Bibi

2
LONER LIFE IN ANOTHER WORLD
COMMENT

― Original Author: **Shoji Goji**

I've read a lot of reviews for the first volume. I saw some saying that they were surprised by how well it came out, or saying things about the original work. It was pretty funny, all in all! One quote I saw said, "Any sane manga artist would've turned this project down." That was really funny! As usual, I'm Shoji Goji, the original author of this work. I've been having a great time reading reviews since the first volume came out. Honestly, Mr. Bibi has done a wonderful job with the story so far (ahaha...). It's a total honor that Mr. Bibi has taken the world I crafted and cranked it up to 11 with visual creativity. Comic Gardo's entire editorial department have put a lot of effort into it too. I'm really pleased with how it's coming along. I look forward to reading more of it, and if you're all happy then I'm happy too! Please keep on reading.